Horrible Harry
Takes the Cake

Horrible Harry
Takes the Cake

BY SUZY KLINE

Pictures by Frank Remkiewicz

SCHOLASTIC INC.

New York Toronto London Auckland Sydney
Mexico City New Delhi Hong Kong Buenos Aires

ISBN-13: 978-0-439-02658-1
ISBN-10: 0-439-02658-X

Text copyright © 2006 by Suzy Kline.
Illustrations copyright © 2006 by Frank Remkiewicz.
All rights reserved. Published by Scholastic Inc., 557 Broadway,
New York, NY 10012, by arrangement with Viking, a division of
Penguin Young Readers Group, a member of Penguin Group
(USA) Inc. SCHOLASTIC and associated logos are trademarks
and/or registered trademarks of Scholastic Inc.

12 11 10 9 8 7 6 5 4 3 2   7 8 9 10 11 12/0

Printed in the U.S.A.   40

First Scholastic printing, April 2007

Set in New Century Schoolbook

Dedicated with all my love
to my beautiful mom, Martha Weaver.
Happy 95th birthday!
Keep loving books!

Special appreciation . . .

to my editor, Catherine Frank, for her valuable help with this story, and to my husband, Rufus, and my daughter, Jennifer, for their thoughtful suggestions. And lastly, a special thank-you to my grandson, Jake DeAngelis, who got me interested in Tasmanian devils.

Contents

Horrible Harry Takes the Cake

The Biggest News

My name is Doug. I'm in third grade. I write stories about my best friend Harry. This one, though, comes with a warning.

Be prepared.

Harry does something really horrible in this story!

It all started when Harry and I walked into Room 3B, and Mary ran up to us. "Did you guys hear the big news?"

Harry threw his winter jacket high up on the shelf. I hung mine on a hanger.

"What's the scoop, Mare?" Harry asked.

She looked like a bubble ready to pop. "Some teacher at South School is . . . *engaged!*"

"How'd you find out, Mary?" ZuZu asked. He was pulling off his winter boots.

"I'm the messenger this week. I go to the office each morning to pick up the teacher's mail. This morning, Mrs. Carpenter, the school secretary, was talking on the phone about a surprise engagement party!"

Harry held up a finger. "Actually, Mare, Doug and I were *there*."

"You were?" Mary exclaimed.

"That engagement party was the shindig in our school library!"

Song Lee and Ida gasped.

Harry explained. "You guys knew something was going on yesterday. Remember how the library was closed and the shades were pulled down? You also knew that my grandmother was bringing a cake after school to that thing."

Everyone nodded their heads.

"Well, while Doug and I were waiting in the hallway and the library door opened . . . bingo! We saw the whole shebang."

"What teacher got engaged?" Song Lee eagerly asked.

Harry flashed a toothy smile. "Ours."

"MISS MACKLE?" everyone shouted.

"The one and only," Harry replied.

Mary sighed, "Ooh! *Miss Mackle's* getting married!"

Song Lee clapped her hands. Mary and Ida danced around the room.

Sidney just grumbled. "I hate weddings. You have to get all dressed up and wear killer shoes. I know. My mom got remarried last year. That's why my last name was changed to LaFleur."

"Who's Miss Mackle marrying?" ZuZu asked.

The girls stopped dancing.

"Yes!" Mary replied, running back to Harry. "Who is Miss Mackle's fiancé?"

"I know that word, fiancé," Sid said. "It's French for the dude who's getting married."

"Don't say 'dude'!" Mary snapped. "Say something else."

"How about . . . the *Groom of Room 3B*?" Harry added with a chuckle. Then he winked at me. I knew he was having some fun.

"Hmmmm," Harry said, tapping his fingertips together. "I'll tell you guys something about the Groom of Room 3B. Miss Mackle was standing next to him at the party. Now, was it the computer teacher, Mr. Skooghammer? The second-grade teacher, Mr. Moulder? Or our music teacher, Mr. Marks?"

I cracked up. Miss Mackle had been standing next to all three, but Harry had no idea which one was the groom!

"So?" Mary demanded. "Which one was it?"

"I'm not spoiling the surprise," Harry said. "Miss Mackle will tell you herself this morning."

Harry and I exchanged a smile.

We couldn't wait to find out either!

"At least we know it's one of three guys," Dexter said. He began singing the wedding march song. "Dum dum de dum, dum dum de dum, dum dum de dum dum, de dum dum de dum."

6

Mary blew up her bangs. She was frustrated. When the bell rang, we raced for our seats.

Moments later we heard footsteps coming down the hall. Everyone looked at the doorway.

"It's a *sub*!" Sid said.

"A substitute teacher," Mary groaned.

Harry sank down in his seat.

"Good morning, boys and girls!" a tall man with wavy hair said. He wrote

"Mr. Flaubert" in cursive on the board. His capital letters had swoopy swirls.

"It's pronounced 'Flow Bear,'" he said. "I'm glad, because I like animals."

And then he smiled.

Investigating
the Animal Kingdom

Harry got a long face. "Where's Miss Mackle?" he blurted out.

"She has a dentist appointment," Mr. Flaubert said.

"Bet she's having a cavity drilled," Sidney replied. "*Bzzzzzzzzzzzzzz!*"

The substitute chuckled. "Well, boys and girls, I thought we could have some fun today doing a project."

"What kind of project?" ZuZu asked.

"Actually, it has something to do with

my old job," the substitute said. "I've been a lawyer for ten years, and now I'm making a career change. I want to be a teacher."

"Why?" Mary asked.

"Because of kids like you."

We all smiled.

"What's the project about?" ZuZu repeated.

"I'd like you to choose one animal, investigate it, and defend its greatness, just like a lawyer would."

"What do you mean 'investigate' the animal?" Sid asked.

Harry answered before the teacher had a chance. "You dig up facts on it, and write 'em down. I know. *I'm* a detective."

Mr. Flaubert smiled as he looked at the seating chart. "Well said, uh . . . Harry."

Harry beamed. "Do we get to pick any animal to *investigate*?" he asked. Harry liked that "I" word.

"Any living creature in the animal kingdom," Mr. Flaubert explained. "For example, someone could even pick the worm and defend its greatness!"

"Worms? Yuck!" Mary exclaimed. "I'm choosing the horse." And she walked over to the library corner and snatched the "H" encyclopedia.

Harry knew his animal right away. "I'm doing the Tasmanian devil."

Mary dropped her encyclopedia. "Harry, that's a horrible animal."

Sidney groaned, and Ida shivered.

"I like your choice, Harry," Mr. Flaubert said. "Looks like there are some students who don't agree with you. Let's see how you defend your animal with good facts."

Harry's smile was toothy. I could tell he liked the challenge. He started drawing a Tasmanian devil. It looked like a really furry rat.

Song Lee reached for the "W" encyclopedia. I think she was going to defend the worm.

I got busy drawing the long nose of a bandicoot.

By the time Harry and I finished drawing our animals, the "T" and "B" encyclopedias were taken. So Harry and I went on our classroom computer. After we got a few good animal facts, we asked to go to the library.

"Good idea, boys," Mr. Flaubert said. "You're using more than one source of information." As soon as he handed us the library pass, we took off down the hall.

"I'm really feeling like a detective today," Harry said. "And you know what, Doug?"

"What?"

"I've got the biggest case ever! I've gotta find out who Miss Mackle is marrying and break the news. Maybe we can find a few clues in the library."

"Yeah," I said. "That's where it all happened."

When we got there, Mrs. Michaelsen was limping over to a bookcase.

"What happened to you?" I asked.

"Oh, I dropped a can of soup on my bare foot last night. It still hurts."

"That's too bad," I said.

"Sore piggies are a bummer," Harry added.

The librarian tried to smile. "What can I do for you boys?"

"I need a book on the bandicoot," I said.

"I need one on the Tasmanian devil." Harry grinned.

"How timely!" Mrs. Michaelsen replied. "I just got a new book in this month called *Australian Marsupials*. You boys can share it."

"No thank you, Mrs. Michaelsen," Harry said politely. "We need *animals*, not *mar-soup-eels*."

The librarian chuckled. "Actually, Harry, mar-sup-i-als *are* animals. Just a special kind. Marsupials have pouches like kangaroos and opossums. That's where they keep their newborn babies for several months. Since the Tasmanian devil and the bandicoot have pouches, they're both marsupials too."

"Cool!" Harry exclaimed. "Bring on the mar-soup-eels, please."

While Mrs. Michaelsen processed the book for checkout, Harry and I snooped around the library.

I had no idea Harry was about to do something *really* horrible!

Harry Takes the Cake

At first, Harry just poked around the wastebasket by the door. "Rats!" he said. "Mr. Beausoleil already picked up the garbage."

When Harry moved the can, he noticed something. "Aha! Cake crumbs!" He pinched a few with his fingers and smelled them. "Orange crumbs from Grandma's carrot cake. Want to smell the spices?"

"No thanks," I said. "I don't want to get crumbs in my nose like you did."

"Better than boogers!" Harry replied.

"Ewweee," I groaned.

Harry laughed as we walked over to the window. Then he spotted something else. "Hmmmm . . . a paper coffee cup and napkin on the windowsill. They both have wedding bells on them." Harry stuffed the napkin in his pocket.

On our way back to the checkout desk, Harry whispered something to me. "Hey, Doug, look what's in that little back room."

I looked through the glass wall.

His grandmother's cake box was on the counter.

Suddenly, Mrs. Michaelsen got up from her computer. "Will you boys excuse me for a minute? I have to go to the office across the hall to get some more book labels."

As soon as the librarian was out of sight, Harry sneaked into the back room.

"No!" I gasped. "You're not supposed to go back there!"

But Harry did!

I leaned over the counter to watch him. My body was frozen like a Popsicle.

That little back room *was* a magical place. There were posters everywhere about reading. Stacks of new books were piled high on a big desk. Sparkly birthday pencils were in a coffee cup. There was a hot plate with a pot of coffee on it. A half-eaten bagel and a container of yogurt sat next to the sink.

I watched Harry lift up the cover of the A-1 Cakes box and hold it open with his head. His hands were doing something inside the box. I couldn't see because Harry's head blocked my view.

"Hurry up, Harry!" I pleaded. "Mrs.

Michaelsen will be back any second!"

Finally, Harry closed the cake box and raced over to me.

"I know who the groom is," he said. "I've got the evidence in my hand." I looked down. Harry was holding something wrapped in that wedding napkin.

"I cut the piece out that has the groom's name on it. Half of the cake was still left. It was a gold mine of information!"

"You stole a piece of cake?" I said. "You could go to prison for that!"

Harry just laughed. "Hey, my grandma made it. The leftovers are just sitting there begging to be eaten. Mrs. Michaelsen likes yogurt, not cake. She won't miss—"

Harry immediately stopped talking

when Mrs. Michaelsen hobbled back into the library.

"Got it," she said, holding up a box of adhesive labels. "Now I can check this book out for you."

Suddenly, I noticed Harry's hair. There was green frosting in it!

I tapped Harry on the shoulder and pointed to his head.

"Nice 'do, huh? Grandma put gel in it this morning."

Mrs. Michaelsen didn't look up. She was too busy sticking the bar code on the back of the book. As soon as she finished, she smoothed some tape over the call number and handed it to us.

I stepped right in front of Harry. I had to block her view of his head.

"Thanks, Mrs. Michaelsen!" I said, and we hurried out the door.

Midway down the hall, I stopped.

"Want to know who the groom is?" Harry asked.

"No!" I said.

Harry took a step back. "No?"

"You've got green frosting in your hair!" I snapped.

Harry put his hand on his head, found the gooey spot, and smeared the frosting around. "Deeeeelicious," he said, licking his fingers. "Do you want a taste?"

"That's gross, Harry," I groaned.

I watched him rinse the gooey part of his hair at the drinking fountain. When we entered the classroom, I didn't wait for him while he stashed the cake in his lunch box. I just hurried back to my seat.

Harry's investigation had gone too far!

Harry's Lunch Box

At noon, Room 3B went to the cafeteria. We have our own lunch table. Usually I sit next to Harry. I didn't today. I sat next to ZuZu and Dexter instead.

Harry was so excited about bringing his lunch box, I don't think he even noticed. He sat next to Mary and Sidney.

"I want everyone's attention," Harry

said, tapping his plastic spoon on the table.

We all looked up.

Harry slowly unfolded the wedding napkin. "This is a piece of Miss Mackle's engagement cake."

Mary stared at the creamy white icing. It had the word "Mark" written in green frosting.

"Mr. Marks!" she shouted.

"Now you know who the Groom of Room 3B is! *And* . . . the world's best detective!" Harry bragged.

Song Lee and Mary clasped their hands. Ida sighed, "The music teacher! She's marrying Mr. Marks!"

"The evidence was on my grandma's cake all along," Harry explained. "Someone just ate the 'Mr.' and the 'S.'"

Mary shot Harry a nasty look. "How

did you happen to get a piece of the engagement cake?"

"Grandma gave Doug and me a sample piece yesterday."

I stared at my buddy. What phony baloney! She did give us a sample piece, but not *that one*!

Mary didn't let Harry off the hook too easily. "Why didn't you show us the piece of cake this morning?"

"Because I wanted to share it at lunch for dessert." Harry took a plastic knife off his lunch tray and started cutting the cake into eight little pieces. Everyone watched him hand one to Song Lee, Mary, Ida, ZuZu, Dexter, Sidney, and me.

As the kids started to eat their pieces of carrot cake, I pushed mine away.

"Can I have it?" Sid asked.

"Every crumb," I muttered. Harry raised his eyebrows.

On our way out to lunch recess, Harry came up to me. "Want to play kickball, Doug?" he asked.

"No," I said. "I don't like playing with a thief."

Harry suddenly looked a little sick.

Defend Your Animal

Harry

Everyone went back to class feeling happy except for Harry and me. I didn't like what he did, but I couldn't tattle on him. Harry was my best friend. Didn't he have a conscience?

I was glad we had to give our animal talks. It got my mind off things for a while.

Mary went first. She walked up to the front of the room and stood behind a podium. Mr. Flaubert had borrowed it from the auditorium.

"Be forceful," he said. "If you believe what you say, others will too."

Mary set some notes down on the podium and got ready to talk. She spoke in a strong voice.

"Horses are great animals. They have a single toe covered by a hoof for fast running. The fastest racehorses can go forty-three miles per hour. They're vegetarians. Their tail is used against nasty insects. They have beau-

tiful manes on their neck. A male horse is called a stallion. A female is called a mare. Their average lifespan is twenty years, but some live to be thirty. Horses are famous in stories like *Black Beauty*, *Fury*, and *The Black Stallion*. If I had a horse, I would call him 'Black Cutey.'"

When she sat down, we clapped.

"It looks like you won your argument," Mr. Flaubert said. "Everyone agrees your animal is a great one! Good job, Mary. Who wants to go next?"

Harry stood up. "I will," he said.

He walked up to the podium and held up a good drawing he had made of the Tasmanian devil. "You're looking at a great animal," he said. "It lives in Australia on an island called Tasmania. That's why we call the animals

Tasmanian devils. They're mar-soup-eels. That means they have pouches like kangaroos and opossums. They hide during the day and hunt for food at night.

"Actually, I'm a lot like the Tasmanian devil. They love meat. I do too. They climb trees. I do too. They give off a bad smell when they're afraid. I blast one when I get nervous."

Lots of kids giggled. I sniffed the air. I thought I smelled something. Did Harry pass gas? Was he nervous?

Harry continued. "But the best thing about Tasmanian devils is that they clean up the land. They eat the leftover meat on dead animal carcasses. That means there are fewer maggots, so Tasmanian devils help prevent diseases among people."

Mary sat up. She liked that reason.

Mr. Flaubert did too. He put two thumbs up.

"The last thing I'm telling you is important. There is a Tasmanian national park. The Tasmanian devils are protected animals. They won't be extinct."

When Harry finished, everyone clapped.

Even Mary. "If they prevent diseases, they're great," she said.

Harry sat down in his seat. He wasn't smiling.

"It smells in here," Sidney said.

It was Harry! He *was* passing gas. Something was bothering him. I crossed

my fingers, hoping it was Harry's conscience.

After Song Lee talked about the worm, and Sidney defended anteaters, Room 3B got a big surprise.

The Groom in Room 3B

"Miss Mackle!" everyone shouted.

"You're here!" Mary said.

The teacher scooted into the room and took off her coat. "Hello, Mr. Flaubert. I hope I'm not interrupting."

"Please join us! We still have more animal talks to share."

"Wonderful! After that I would like to share some news myself."

Mary immediately whispered, "Act like you don't know."

Song Lee and Ida nodded.

Dexter and ZuZu nodded too.

"Somebody cut the cheese again," Sidney complained.

"It was probably *you*, Sid!" Mary scolded. "Don't you know you're not supposed to call attention to things like that?"

Sid didn't say anything more. He just waved his hand in front of his nose.

I kept my fingers crossed that it was the Tasmanian devil in our room.

After listening to talks on the toucan, the monkey, the boa constrictor, the hummingbird, the bat, the yellow-spotted river turtle, the porcupine, the sloth, and my bandicoot, Miss Mackle went to the podium herself.

"Bravo, class! What an outstanding job you did in defending your animals.

They're all great—just like you! Now, I have some good news to share. I'm getting married!"

Everyone cheered and clapped.

Mary and Ida giggled. I could tell it was hard for them to pretend they didn't know.

"I like your ring," Song Lee said in a soft voice. She could see the best because she was sitting right in front of the teacher. "It has three beautiful diamonds."

"For Room 3B," Miss Mackle replied with a big smile.

We all oohed.

Then Miss Mackle dropped the bomb! "I'm going to marry Mark Flaubert."

The room turned pin-quiet.

Mary glared at Harry.

Everyone stared at the substitute teacher.

"You're h-him?" Sid stammered.

"I'm the lucky guy!" Mr. Flaubert said.

Mary groaned, "Harry Spooger, you're the world's worst detective!"

Harry slowly shook his head. He couldn't believe it.

Dexter started humming the wedding song again. "Dum dum de dum, dum dum de dum, dum dum de dum dum, de dum dum de dum."

Lots of kids gathered around Miss Mackle to get a closer look at her engagement ring.

I walked over to Harry. His eyes were watery.

"I'm not going to tell, Harry," I said. "But what you did was wrong."

Harry put his head down on his desk. I could tell his conscience had zapped him.

When I looked up, Mrs. Michaelsen was standing in the doorway. She had the big white cake box in her arms!

A Piece of Cake

"Miss Mackle!" the librarian said, setting the cake box down on the table. "I saved the leftover pieces of cake for your class like you asked, but I'm afraid the 'Mark' piece got eaten by mistake."

Six people looked at Harry.

Before Mary had a chance to tattle, Harry stood up. "It was me," he said. "I took it."

Miss Mackle looked worried. "Harry? How could that be?"

Mrs. Michaelsen immediately wiggled her finger. "I think I know. Come along, Harry. We need to talk."

"You look like you swallowed a canary, Harry!" Sid said.

No one laughed as Harry followed the librarian to the door.

"I'm really sorry, Mrs. Michaelsen,"

he moaned. "I couldn't help it. I'm a detective. It was a piece of important evidence."

Miss Mackle and Mr. Flaubert exchanged a look.

Me?

I was relieved! Harry did the right thing. He told the truth. Now I could finally enjoy a piece of that cake!

Harry? He had to stay after school. He told me later he had to wash every table in the library and sweep the floor. He also had to write a letter of apology to Mrs. Michaelsen and to Miss Mackle. The next day he read it to our class.

We sure did a lot of investigating that day, and certainly discovered what's great about twenty animals.

But I have to say the most important thing I learned was *what's great* about my friend Harry. He does have a good conscience.

It may be a smelly one, but it works.

Room 3B's
Animal Facts

Harry

Anteaters
by Sidney LaFleur

1. Anteaters love to eat termites.

2. Anteaters have no teeth.

3. Anteaters have awesome tongues. They can be two feet long!

4. Anteaters can flick their tongue 150 times a minute. That's hard. I tried it.

5. They live in Central and South America.

6. They are called "Stinkers of the Forest" because when they go to the bathroom it really smells.

7. They can weigh as much as I do. Seventy pounds! Sometimes more!

TASMANIAN DEVILS
by Harry Spooger

1. TDs live in Tasmania.
2. TDs are marsupials. They have pouches like kangaroos.
3. TDs love meat. I do too.
4. TDs climb trees. I do too.
5. TDs give off a bad smell when they are nervous. I do too.
6. TDs eat any leftover meat on a dead carcass. That means there are fewer maggots and less disease because of them.
7. There is a national park where TDs are protected to prevent them from ever going extinct.
8. TDs hunt for their own food at night and hide during the day.

Worms
by Song Lee Park

1. Worms have no eyes, arms, or legs.
2. They need moist soil.
3. The largest earthworm was twenty-two feet long. It was found in South Africa.
4. Worms like to make tunnels in the soil. They help gardens breathe.
5. Worms ooze out nitrogen. That helps plants grow.
6. Worms can grow a new tail.
7. They are smart too. The University of Michigan did research on worms. They trained them to go through mazes.
8. If you see a worm on the sidewalk after the rain, please don't step on it.

Bandicoots
by Doug Hurtuk

1. Bandicoots are marsupials. They have pouches to carry their young.
2. Their faces are long and pointed.
3. Bandicoots eat insects, roots, fruits, and veggies.
4. Bandicoots attack their enemies by jumping on their rear end.
5. Bandicoots live in Australia, Tasmania, and New Guinea.
6. They can hop like kangaroos because they have long back legs.

Horses
by Mary Berg

1. Horses have a single toe covered by a hoof.
2. The fastest racehorses go forty-three miles per hour.
3. A male horse is called a stallion. A female is called a mare.
4. A foal is a baby horse.
5. A foal is called a yearling after its first birthday.
6. A filly is a young female horse. A colt is a young male horse.
7. The average horse's lifespan is twenty years.
8. A horse's height is measured in hands. A hand is four inches long.
9. Horses are famous in stories like <u>Black Beauty</u>, <u>Fury</u>, and <u>The Black Stallion</u>.
10. Horses are vegetarians.

Tarantulas
by Ida Burrell

1. Tarantulas are the biggest spiders.
2. They can be the size of a dinner plate or a dime.
3. They have eight hairy legs.
4. Their fangs have venom but it's not deadly to humans.
5. They can eat insects, rodents, and small birds.
6. They like to hide.
7. They can live in rain forests and deserts.
8. Tarantulas in Australia can whistle! They rub their mouth hairs together to make whistling sounds. They whistle to scare their enemies away.

Hound Dogs
by Dexter Doby

1. Elvis sang "You ain't nothin' but a hound dog" in the song "Hound Dog."
2. Hound dogs came from France.
3. They are actually basset hounds.
4. They are big dogs on small legs.
5. They are scent dogs. Their nose is close to the ground. They like to smell everything. Even dirty socks in your laundry basket!
6. George Washington had three hound dogs in his house. He named them Tarter, True Love, and Sweet Lips!
7. They have sad eyes and velvety ears.
8. Don't pick up a hound dog under his chest. You might hurt him because he's so long! Pick up the whole dog in your arms carefully.